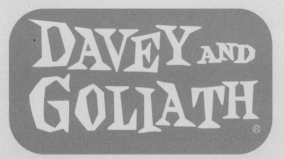

THE KITE

Adapted by Sue Wright from the original episode

SCHOLASTIC INC.

New York   Toronto   London   Auckland   Sydney
Mexico City   New Delhi   Hong Kong   Buenos Aires

ISBN 0-439-69831-6

Copyright © 2005 Evangelical Lutheran Church in America.
Davey and Goliath ® and Davey and Goliath characters are registered trademarks of the Evangelical Lutheran Church in America.
All rights reserved.
Published by Scholastic Inc.
SCHOLASTIC and associated logos are trademarks and/or registered trademarks of Scholastic Inc.

Designed by Rick DeMonico

12 11 10 9 8 7 6 5 4 3 2 1   5 6 7 8 9/0

Printed in Singapore
First printing, February 2005

Davey and his buddies huddled together on the playground after school.

"Anybody want to play baseball?" Tommy asked hopefully.

"Sure," answered Davey. "But before we choose teams, let's see if the new boy wants to play."

"I guess, but if he does, he has to be on your team," said Tommy. "I don't want some stranger on my team."

Seeing the new boy sitting by himself made Davey feel sad. The boy looked lonely.

"We're going to play baseball," Davey told him. "Want to play?"

"Okay," the boy replied.

"Great! My name is Davey. What's yours?"

"Teddy," said the new boy.

Davey introduced the new boy to his friends.
"Guys, meet Teddy, my new left fielder."
Teddy grinned. "Gee, thanks, Davey. I promise
I won't let you down."

By the last inning, Davey's team led Tommy's by a single run.

"Three strikes and we win," yelled Davey's friend Jimmy. "Give it all you've got, Davey."

"I'll try. But be ready! Jack can hit the ball a mile," Davey called back.

On the next pitch, Jack hit the baseball — hard. It soared into the sky and straight for left field.

"Oh, no!" shouted Jimmy. "It's headed for the new boy."

Teddy raced to catch the ball. When it fell into his glove, the team whooped. "We won!" they cried.

"That was one swell catch," Jimmy said. "You saved us, Teddy."

"Saved us for sure," echoed Davey. "Say, want to come over to my house this afternoon? I'll introduce you to my dog, Goliath. And you can help Jimmy and me finish our kite."

"You really want me to?" Teddy asked.
"Why not, come on!" said Davey.

The moment Goliath spotted Davey, his tail began to wag out of control.

Davey laughed. "I'm glad to see you, too, Goliath. Now settle down and shake hands with my new friend, Teddy. Teddy, this is Goliath."

Teddy stuck out his hand. But instead of shaking hands, Goliath gave Teddy a wet, slobbery lick. "Yuck," Teddy complained. "Does your dog always treat new people this way?"

Davey laughed. "Only if he likes them. Isn't that right, Goliath?"

Goliath nodded, even though he thought Davey's new friend acted rather peculiar.

In a few minutes, the boys were running out of Davey's garage and into the sunshine. Their handsome new kite trailed behind them.

"Wow, what a kite!" Jimmy crowed. "All we need is more string and she's ready to fly."

"Hold on and I'll find some," offered Davey.

"Before you go, better check out Goliath,"
Teddy jeered. "That leftover sticky paper
is driving him crazy."
Jimmy giggled. "He's wiggling all over."

"Be careful, old boy," cautioned Davey. "One more step and..."

"Too late," moaned Teddy.

"Our kite is torn to pieces," groaned Jimmy. "And we didn't even have a chance to fly it."

Davey sighed. "Oh, Goliath, what have you done?"

"I'm sorry," Goliath said. He spoke in a special voice only Davey could hear.

"Don't worry," Davey whispered. "I forgive you, Goliath."

Teddy exploded. "You forgive him? How can you forgive Goliath when he's ruined our kite?"

Davey looked at Teddy seriously. "I have to forgive Goliath, Teddy. I love him. Besides, we've got plenty of material to make another kite."

So the three boys got to work. They cut paper and tape and string. Half an hour later, their new kite was ready to go.

"Where's Goliath?" asked Davey as the new kite bobbed higher and higher in the air. "He should see this."

"He's over there," said Teddy. "In the bushes."

"In the bushes?" Davey asked.

"Yes, and he better stay there. We don't want him ruining *this* kite," Teddy said.

"He isn't going to ruin our kite," protested Davey.

"He might," said Teddy. "Scram, dog."

Goliath sidled up to Davey, ignoring Teddy.

"Your new friend isn't very sociable," Goliath observed mournfully.

Davey gave Goliath a comforting pat.

Jimmy passed the kite to Teddy. "Your turn," he said. "But don't let out all of the string. We still owe Davey a turn."

"He'll get a turn after I see just how high this kite can go," Teddy declared.

"Yeah, well, I'm telling you, don't forget about Davey!" said Jimmy.

With that, Teddy began running as fast as he could. But he didn't notice the tree standing in his path. The string became tangled in the tree, and a minute later, the kite was dangling from the telephone lines.

"You've broken our kite," Jimmy exclaimed. "And just because you wouldn't share. Go home, Teddy. You aren't welcome here anymore."

"If that's the way you feel," shouted Teddy, "I'm glad I broke your kite." He ran away as fast as he could.

Davey and Jimmy went back to the garage and started making another new kite.

"If we hurry," Davey said, "we can test her out before supper."

Those kids never give up, thought Goliath. He was full of admiration.

Watching their new kite sail into the breeze,
Davey and Jimmy wondered if it could possibly
sail all the way to heaven. It sure was one peach
of a kite.

"Thank goodness Teddy isn't here to break it,"
said Jimmy.

"Don't speak too soon," warned Davey. "I think I see Teddy sneaking around behind those trees."

Jimmy gasped. "It *is* Teddy!"

"Maybe he's come back to apologize," suggested Davey.

"Not likely," grumbled Jimmy. "Teddy, go home!" he shouted into the trees.

"But I'm sorry," Teddy shouted back. "Will you forgive me?"

"Did you say forgive?" asked Jimmy.

"Yes, like Davey forgave Goliath," Teddy answered.

"Hey, that was different, Teddy," Jimmy said. "Goliath didn't ruin our kite by being selfish like you!"

"Perhaps we should forgive Teddy," Davey said
slowly. "God would forgive him."

Jimmy looked doubtful. "God would forgive Teddy?
Even after he was so mean?"

"You know God would, Jimmy. God loves us and forgives us, no matter what," Davey replied.

"Well, I guess I can forgive him, if you and God can," said Jimmy.

"Hey, Teddy! Get over here," Davey and Jimmy
called. "Don't be afraid. We won't hurt you."
Teddy couldn't believe his ears. The boys seemed
to have changed their minds about him.

"Does that mean you forgive me?" asked Teddy.
"Absolutely," said Davey. "And to prove it, take
another turn with the kite."

"Thanks," said Teddy. "But Davey, look at your dog. He's covered in sticky paper again. You fly the kite. I'll help Goliath."

Teddy bent down and pulled the sticky paper away from Goliath's fur. "There you go," he murmured. "That paper can't bother you anymore. Stay now, boy, and help us fly our beautiful kite."

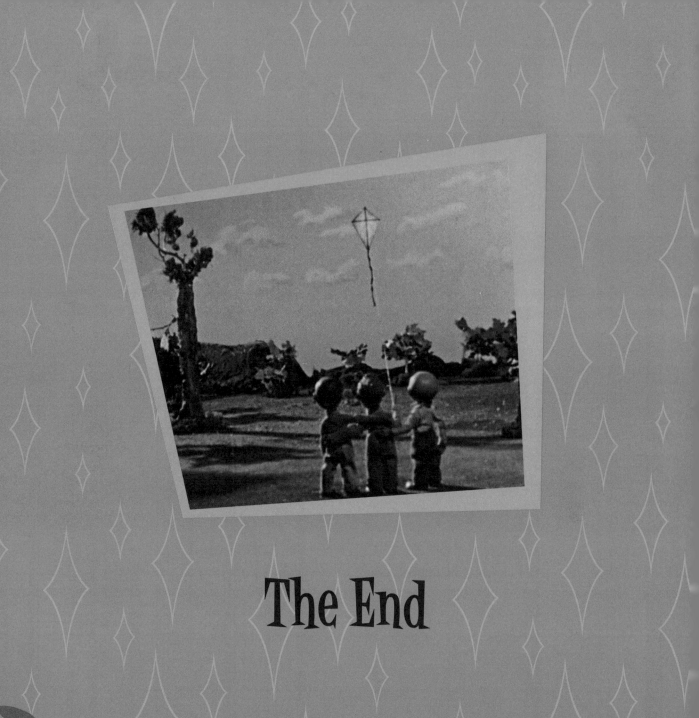

The End